Rudy Rides the Rails

A DEPRESSION ERA STORY

BY DANDI DALEY MACKALL
ILLUSTRATED BY CHRIS ELLISON

To Rambling Rudy, a gentleman hobo who rode the rails during the Great Depression, was crowned "King of the Hoboes" in 1986, and "caught the Westbound" in 2004.

DANDI

In memory of my great grandmother Maggie Worsham, who always responded with kindness to the hoboes that knocked on her door.

CHRIS

Text Copyright © 2007 Dandi Daley Mackall
Illustration Copyright © 2007 Chris Ellison

Sleeping Bear Press

310 North Main Street, Suite 300
Chelsea, MI 48118
www.sleepingbearpress.com

© 2007 Thomson Gale, a part of the Thomson Corporation.

Thomson, Star Logo and Sleeping Bear Press are trademarks and Gale is a registered trademark used herein under license.

Printed and bound in China.

First Edition

10 9 8 7 6 5 4 3 2 1

Library of Congress Cataloging-in-Publication Data

Mackall, Dandi Daley.
Rudy rides the rails : a Depression era story / by Dandi Daley
Mackall ; illustrated by Chris Ellison.
p. cm.
Summary: In 1932, during the Depression in Ohio, thirteen-year-old
Rudy, determined to help his family weather the hard times, hops a
train going west to California and experiences the hobo life.
ISBN 10: 1-58536-286-7
ISBN 13: 978-1-58536-286-8
[1. Tramps—Fiction. 2. Railroads trains—Fiction. 3. Depressions
—1929—Fiction.]   I. Ellison, Chris, ill. II. Title.
PZ7.M1905Rud 2007
[Fic]—dc22   2006023431

AUTHOR'S NOTE

In 1929, the end of "the Roaring Twenties," many Americans believed they had good reason to sing and dance. Farmers had been producing more and more crops, and industry sprouted factories throughout the United States.

But there were problems, too. Prices of farm products began to drop. Dust storms blackened skies from Texas to the Dakotas, and as far east as Washington, D.C. People stopped buying goods that the increasing number of factories produced. Companies went out of business and couldn't pay their loans.

On "Black Tuesday," October 29, 1929, the stock market crashed, and banks ran out of money. Millionaires lost millions. Average Americans lost everything they had. It was America's worst crisis since the Civil War and became known as the Great Depression. In Ohio, half of the workers in Cleveland lost jobs, 60% in Akron, and 80% in Toledo.

A quarter of a million teenagers left their homes to ride the rails as hoboes, in search of a better life. They were met with the same mixed reactions as our twenty-first-century homeless—ridicule and cruelty, along with the understanding and kindness of strangers.

My dad grew up close to the railroad tracks in Hamilton, Missouri. During the Depression, hoboes would stop and ask for a bite to eat. My grandmother always gave them something and wondered how they knew to stop at her house...until she found the smiling cat carved into the big oak on the front lawn.

I met the real "Ramblin' Rudy," Rudy Phillips, in 2000. My story is a work of fiction, but I hope it captures Rudy's spirit and the spirit of American adventure lived by young Rudy and so many others during the Great Depression.

1932 was a time when America forgot how to smile. Drought turned the middle of the nation into "the Dustbowl." Corn and wheat prices fell so low that farmers left their crops in the field to rot. Banks ran out of money, and schools closed their doors. Fathers lost their jobs, and mothers had no food to put on the table for hungry children.

Rudy Phillips believed the whole world had changed.

And nobody had changed more than Rudy's pa.

Rudy tried to see around the line of men and boys winding ahead of him, clear to the boarded-up gate of the rubber plant. Everybody had hit on hard times.

Up ahead, people drifted out of line as word filtered down: "Nobody's hiring today."

Rudy shuffled home through the snow, wishing he had more than cardboard soles in his shoes. Pa was sitting on the porch step, looking as if all the hope had drained out of his bones. Rudy could remember when the front porch had been filled with Ma's singing and Pa's banjo playing. But when Pa lost his job, the music got lost, too.

"You gotta look out for you and yours, and nobody else." That's what Pa taught Rudy. But now Pa couldn't even take care of his own. Ma sneaked out to stand in the relief line for cold beans and moldy cheese, while Rudy's little sisters waited at soup kitchen and mission back doors. Pa pretended not to know.

In the distance, Rudy heard the lonesome whistle of a train. Hundreds of teens no older than Rudy had hopped the B&O line out of Akron, Ohio, bound for lumbering forests in the north or fields ripe for harvesting to the west and south. They rode the rails to as far off as California, where orange trees grew in every yard and dreams had a chance of coming true.

"I'm going West," Rudy announced. When his pa didn't answer, Rudy pressed on. "I'll find work and send money home."

Ma cried and tried to talk him out of it. When she couldn't, she tied up a bundle, with a chunk of cheese, a loaf end of bread, and all she had, $2.10. Then she kissed her son goodbye. Rudy figured that even if he didn't strike it rich in California, there'd be one less mouth to feed.

Rudy crouched in the weeds by the railroad yards. An outbound jerked onto the tracks like an iron snake, smoke puffing from its nostrils. A sliver of moonlight lit an open boxcar. Rudy jumped and grasped the grab iron to pull himself up. Then he rolled onto the boxcar floor. The whistle howled, and Rudy Phillips was on his way.

Inside the boxcar it was black as coal and twice as dusty. The floorboards shook like chattering teeth and smelled like sourdough gone bad. But as Rudy watched the yards grow smaller and smaller, he knew "Cali" was getting closer and closer.

Something stirred behind him. Rudy imagined rats the size of Ohio. He wheeled around to see a small circle of glowing red fire. Rudy wanted to jump from the train, but it swayed and bucked, and he couldn't stand up.

Rudy stared into the blackness until two figures took shape. One was bone thin and so tall he had to bend over. "Name's Fishbones," the man said. "This here's Boxcar Betty." Rudy saw now that the glowing circle was the tip of the old woman's cigar. She laughed, and Rudy thought of the witch's cackle in *Hansel and Gretel*. "You caught yourself a rattler, Sonny!" she declared.

It didn't take Rudy long to understand why the train was called a "rattler." It shook him like dice in a cup. Still, he was pretty sure that his insides would have been rattling, even if the train hadn't been. What if he'd made a mistake getting on this freight? The biggest mistake of his life.

"What's your handle?" Fishbones asked.

"I'm Rudy," he answered. Pa's warning popped into his head: Look out for you and yours, and nobody else. Rudy curled up in the far corner of the boxcar and pretended to get some shut-eye. Finally, he did fall asleep, to the clickety clack and the sway of the track.

"Bulls ahead!"

Rudy woke with a start, surprised to see himself covered with newspaper.

"I'll take my Hoover blanket back now," Betty said, reaching for the paper.

Lots of folks blamed President Hoover for the Great Depression. Rudy handed back the Hoover blanket, wondering why she'd bothered covering him. "What kinda bulls?"

Fishbones pointed down the track to a handful of uniformed police, just waiting for them.

"Jump!" Fishbones hollered.

Rudy stared at the iron rails racing below. He closed his eyes and jumped. Two bulls were racing toward him.

Rudy took off running like lightning on fire.

When Rudy stopped to catch his breath, Fishbones appeared from behind a bush. "All clear," he said.

Boxcar Betty walked up. "Come on! I know a place we can get us a sitdown."

Rudy knew most hoboes went asking for food, but he could look out for himself. "Naw, I better git walkin'." He followed the tracks alone until he found a diner. Rudy ordered bacon, eggs, toast, and pancakes. With only a dollar of Ma's money left, he knew he had to find work.

Rudy tried seven places before he found a nickel flop that would let him sweep up for a dime a day. After six weeks in Chicago, "the Big Town," he had enough saved to send three dollars back home.

But the whistle was calling him. That night Rudy caught a freight on the fly, bound for the West.

In Freeport, Illinois, the train was met by farmers holding up signs that read, "Field Work! 10 cents an hour."

Rudy dug and planted from dawn until dark. When he thought he was too tired to lift the hoe one more time, he'd imagine what his ma would do when she got the money in the mail. He could picture her buying a chicken and surprising Pa and the girls with it. Or shoes. Maybe there'd be enough for her to get new shoes.

After a week in the fields, Rudy had spent half his wages filling the hole in his stomach. He sent the rest of the money home, then hopped a freight that was so full of hoboes he had to stand all the way to Dubuque, Iowa.

At a little whistle stop in Waterloo, when the other hoboes split up to panhandle near the tracks, Rudy was too hungry not to try it himself. He knocked at a cottage with flower beds. A woman came to the door, took one look at him, and slammed the door in his face. Rudy tried a big house, a rundown shack, and a house with a picket fence. Nobody gave him so much as a crust of bread.

When he got back to the boxcar, every other hobo was feasting. Rudy wondered how they could always pick the friendliest places. But he didn't ask. It was hard just looking out for himself.

In Britt, Iowa, a dozen hoboes got on and a dozen got off. Rudy spotted Fishbones and fell in a distance behind him, hoping Fishbones might lead him to a friendly house. Instead, Boxcar Betty showed up, and they ducked into the thick brush. Rudy followed farther and farther, winding through burnt-out cornfields, where dead stalks hung their empty heads. Rudy was afraid he'd never find his way out.

Rudy heard music. It had been so long since he'd heard singing that he stopped dead in his tracks. For a minute, he was back home on his own front porch, with Pa strumming and Ma singing, the smell of honeysuckle mixing with the promise of apple pie from the oven.

"Caught you!" A giant arm, thick as Rudy's leg, lifted him off the ground.

Fishbones came to the rescue. "Easy, Moose! This here's Ramblin' Rudy."

The man let go, and Rudy sprawled to the ground. "Welcome to the Jungle, Ramblin' Rudy!" he bellowed.

Rudy grinned. He finally had his very own handle, and he liked the sound of it.

Boxcar Betty led Rudy to a blazing bonfire and Rudy smelled something that made his mouth water.

"Mulligan Stew," Boxcar explained. "But you got to put something in to take something out." She grinned, showing two missing teeth. "Wanna come with us to get grub?"

Rudy thought about Pa's warning to look out for himself. But he didn't want to get another door slammed in his face. His stomach ached for food he didn't know how to get. And that's all there was to it. Sometimes a fella did need somebody besides himself.

Rudy nodded. "I reckon I'd like that."

Fishbones led the way. They came to a nice, brick house, and Rudy could see a kindly-looking woman inside. "Here?"

Fishbones shook his head and pointed to a sign carved into the tree. It looked like a rectangle with a jagged line through it. "A bad-tempered woman," he said. Rudy didn't understand.

At the next house Boxcar Betty pointed out a sign scratched into the porch, a rectangle with a dot. "Danger," she whispered.

"Who left the signs?" Rudy asked, hurrying to keep up.

"Hoboes looking out for each other," Fishbones answered. He stopped and pointed to a big oak tree.

Rudy took a closer look. "It's a smiling cat."

Fishbones winked. "And it means we'll find kindness here."

Sure enough, a smiling woman came to the door. "Have a seat on the porch," she offered. "I'll see what I can find."

Back in front of the bonfire, Rudy felt pretty proud as he handed over cabbage, a turkey leg, and three potatoes for the pot. He wished his pa could have felt what he was feeling. Mulligan stew turned out to be the best meal Ramblin' Rudy had ever eaten, although he'd never tell Ma that. When nobody could eat another bite, Fishbones began a tune on his harmonica. Texas Slim beat on a frying pan. Pretty soon, Guitar Charlie and Banjo Bill joined in. Rudy closed his eyes and imagined he was back on his own front porch—before the world changed.

After that, Ramblin' Rudy learned from the hoboes he met. In Nebraska, when he tried to ride the "cowcatcher," the engine grate, cinders burned his eyes until "Shorty" Simms taught him to tie his bindle kerchief over his eyes. He rode the "blinds," the platform between connecting cars, through the Rockies and listened to "Preacher" Jones's stories about mountain men. Rudy climbed the roof to "catch the blue" through Utah and Nevada and wondered if the same sky, blue as his baby sister's eyes, reached all the way back to Akron.

Then one morning, Rudy woke to the sight of blue on blue—the Pacific Ocean stretching to the sky. He wished his folks could have seen it.

But as the U.P. chugged into the yards, Rudy could see that there were more hoboes than grains of sand in California. And all of them were looking for work.

It didn't take long for Rudy to discover Cali wasn't the place for him. If they'd had orange trees for everybody, they'd run out before Rudy got there. After odd-jobbing it for a spell, he knew what he wanted, what he needed—home. Before setting out, he got himself a good night's sleep at the "Sally," the Salvation Army. Come morning, Rudy Phillips would be heading home!

Rudy caught the eastbound and started working his way back. There were no smiling cats in the burning Arizona desert. Sunlight attacked through the slats of the boxcar and liked to bake him, until Frisco Fred showed him how to tie a wet kerchief around his neck.

Rudy swept a saloon in Albuquerque, painted a church east of Dodge City, Kansas, washed windows, unloaded fruit, and chopped wood. He saved every penny. In the evenings, he found the sign of the smiling cat. He even got himself a sitdown in Casey from a woman who wasn't just looking out for herself.

Rudy had five dollars in his pocket when the B&O pulled into the Akron yards, past a long line outside the rubber plant. He ran all the way home, stopping only when he reached his front porch. Rudy could imagine music here.

Suddenly, he knew what he had to do. He got out his pocketknife, and into the porch he carved a smiling cat. Rudy stepped back and smiled at his hobo sign. From now on, folks who passed by would know they'd find kindness in the home of Ramblin' Rudy.

A HOBO GLOSSARY

B&O: Baltimore and Ohio Railroad line; hoboes sometimes called it "Bum's Own."

billy club: short, wooden club or bat, carried by policemen

bindle: hobo's bundle or bag

blind: the space between the engine and the baggage car, where some hoboes rode

bull: railroad policeman

Cali: California

cannonball: fast freight train

Casey: Kansas City, Missouri

catch a train: to board or hop on a train

catch the Westbound: to die

catching the blue: enjoying a boxcar view of open skies

cowcatcher: the grate on the front of a train's engine

divisions: main freight yards, usually 500 miles apart

grab iron: a bar on the boxcar, where a hobo would grab when jumping aboard

hobo: someone who wanders from place to place; hoboes frequently caught rides on freight trains in the Depression. The term may have come from a call used by railway mail handlers in the 1880s: "Ho, boy!" Or it may have come from migrant workers who showed up for work carrying their own hoes—hoe boys.

Hoover blanket: newspaper used as a blanket, so named because many blamed then-President Herbert Hoover for the bad economy.

Hoover hotel: sleeping outside, with a newspaper for shelter

jungle: a hobo camp

Mulligan stew: hobo stew, made of anything and everything

nickel flop: an all-night movie house

rattler: bumpy train

rods: bars beneath a freight

Sally: the Salvation Army

a sitdown (or set down): taking a full meal inside somebody's home

U.P.: Union Pacific Railroad

whistle stop: a stop in a division to change crews

Symbol	Meaning	Symbol	Meaning	Symbol	Meaning
◯	Nothing gained	⊗	Good place for a handout	⌁	Ill-tempered woman
◯→	Go this way	⚋	Work available	🐱	Kindness here
🚂	Good place to catch a train	✕	Safe camp	▽	Road spoiled
✕	OK, all right	⊔	Camp here	⋀	A sitdown meal
◇◇	Keep quiet	▭•	Danger	⊓	Here is the place